Weiss, Nicki
Chuckie

Chuckie

by
NICKI WEISS

GREENWILLOW BOOKS
New York

Library of Congress Cataloging in Publication Data
Weiss, Nicki. Chuckie.
Summary: A good little girl starts misbehaving
when her baby brother arrives, but has a
change of attitude when he says his first word.
[1. Babies—Fiction.   2. Brothers and sisters—
Fiction.   3. Behavior—Fiction]   I. Title.
PZ7.W448145Ch   [E]   81-6323
ISBN-0-688-00670-1   AACR2
ISBN 0-688-00671-X (lib. bdg.)

For Geri

Once there was a little girl named Lucy.

Lucy was a good girl who made her bed,

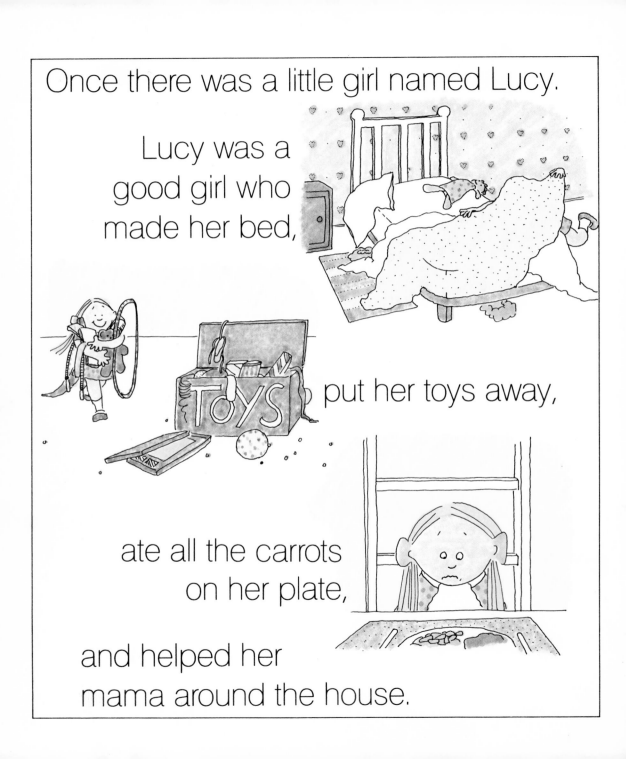

put her toys away,

ate all the carrots on her plate,

and helped her mama around the house.

She said "Please"

 and "Thank you"

and smiled when people said,
   "Oooh, aaah, isn't she cute?"

Then one day
Chuckie came.

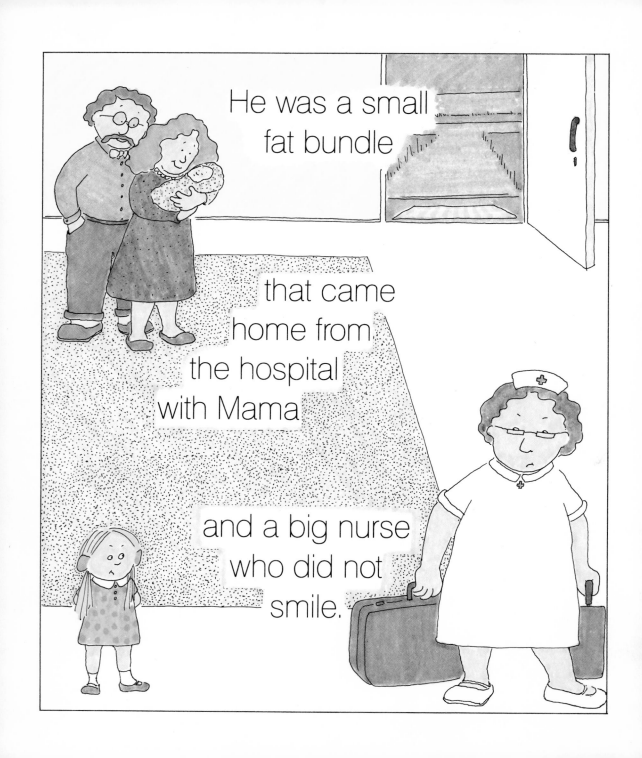

"Oooh, aaah,
isn't he cute?"
said Mama.

"Oooh, aaah,
isn't he cute?"
said Papa.

"Oooh, aaah,
isn't he cute?"
said the nurse.

"Uch," said Lucy.

At first Lucy thought that if she wished hard enough, Chuckie would go away.

But then she would sneak a look under the baby blanket, and Chuckie would still be there.

Then she saw
the nurse packing
her bags.

Whoopee, Lucy said to herself,
Chuckie's going back.

But the big nurse
left and Chuckie
stayed.

And stayed.

For a time Lucy pretended that Chuckie wasn't there.

Mama would walk into the living room holding Chuckie, and Lucy would say, "I bet it's boring to carry a bag of potatoes all the time."

He grew a little fuzz on the top of his head and Lucy said, "Look, Papa, I think that Chuckie has some disease."

Chuckie began to eat food from a spoon and Lucy said, "Better watch it, Mama, or he'll eat all the food in the house."

Chuckie would wake up early in the morning and stare at his mobile

and Lucy would stand in the doorway and say, "Quiet, squirt, or you'll wake the whole house."

Poor Chuckie.

He was not exactly Lucy's idea of fun,
but he did not seem to notice.

He dribbled
his food

when
she walked
into the kitchen.

He made noises

when she
walked out.

If Lucy yelled for her papa, he would gurgle.

If she took a cookie out of his hand, he would giggle.

"Oooh, aaah, isn't he cute?" said Papa.

"Oooh, aaah, isn't he cute?" said Mama.

He's just a dumb lump of baby, Lucy thought.

Things were different since
Chuckie had come.

Lucy left her
bed unmade,

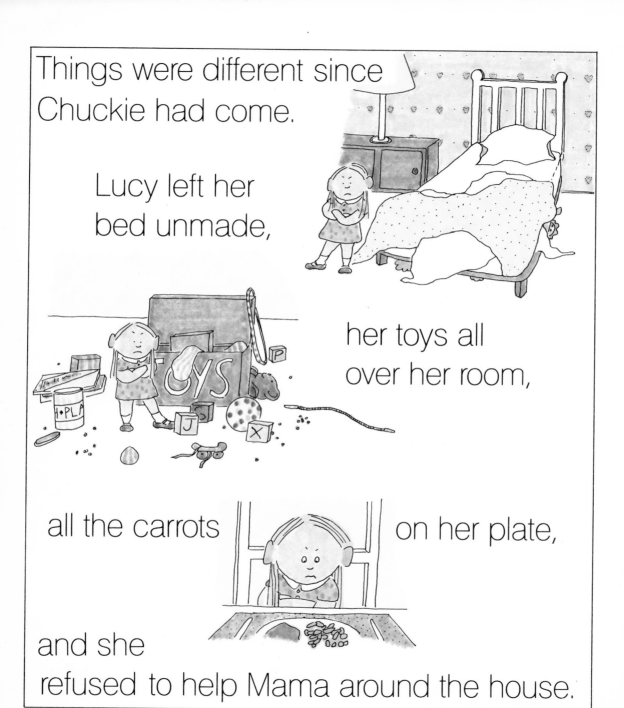

her toys all
over her room,

all the carrots   on her plate,

and she
refused to help Mama around the house.

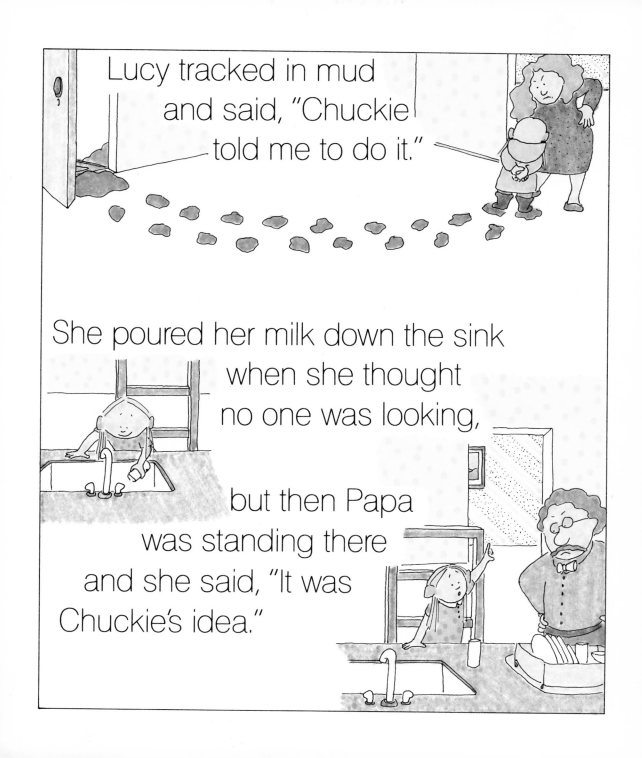

Lucy tracked in mud and said, "Chuckie told me to do it."

She poured her milk down the sink when she thought no one was looking,

but then Papa was standing there and she said, "It was Chuckie's idea."

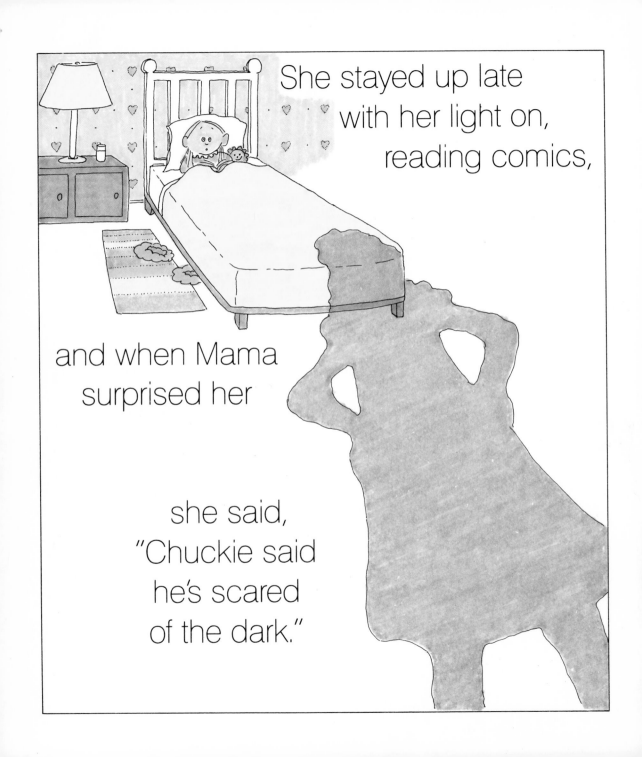

She stayed up late
with her light on,
reading comics,

and when Mama
surprised her

she said,
"Chuckie said
he's scared
of the dark."

Chuckie grew and grew and the fuzz on his head turned to golden ringlets.

Lucy liked to pull those ringlets.

She thought that would make Chuckie cry.

But he only got hiccoughs from laughing.

At night Lucy would tiptoe
into Chuckie's room and
make scary faces.

She'd flip on the light

and say
BOOO!

And Chuckie would
giggle and giggle.

Chuckie began to
sit up in his crib.

Lucy would come
and push
him over.

"Baby,"
she would say.

And Chuckie would
sit right up again
to play some more.

"I think Chuckie likes you a lot," Mama said.

"I think so, too," said Papa.

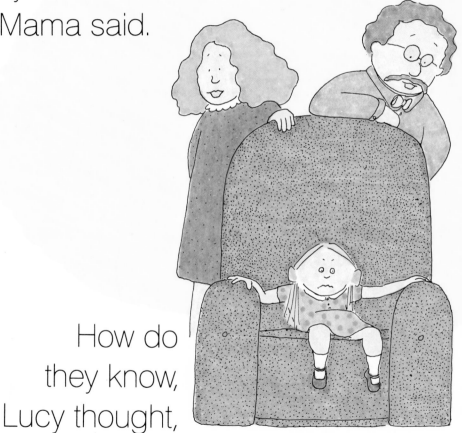

How do they know, Lucy thought,

Chuckie doesn't talk.

Nothing Lucy did seemed to bother Chuckie.
Nothing.

"Oooh, aaah,
isn't he cute?"
said Mama.

"Oooh, aaah,
isn't he cute?"
said Papa.

And then one night at the dinner table
Chuckie began to gurgle. He said,

"Googaa"   "Noonoo"   "Blachhh."

and   and

Mama said,   Papa said, "Sssh!
"He's talking!"   Let's hear what
                 his first word
                 will be!"

"Oh, I'm sure it will be Mama," said Mama.

"But it certainly will be Papa," said Papa.

"Mama!" said Mama.

"Papa!" said Papa.

Lucy took a scoop of ice cream from Chuckie's dish.

Chuckie just giggled and said,

"Pkat" and "Plopf" and "Rszrszrsz"

and giggled some more.

"Papa," said Papa.

"Mama," said Mama.

"Oooh, aaah, isn't he cute?" they said.

Lucy took another scoop from Chuckie's dish.

Just then Chuckie coughed.

Then he began to gurgle.

 "Listen," said Mama.

"Sssh," said Papa.

 "Lucy," said Chuckie.

From that night on, things were different.

Lucy made
her bed.

She put her
toys away,

ate her carrots,

and helped her
mama around the house.

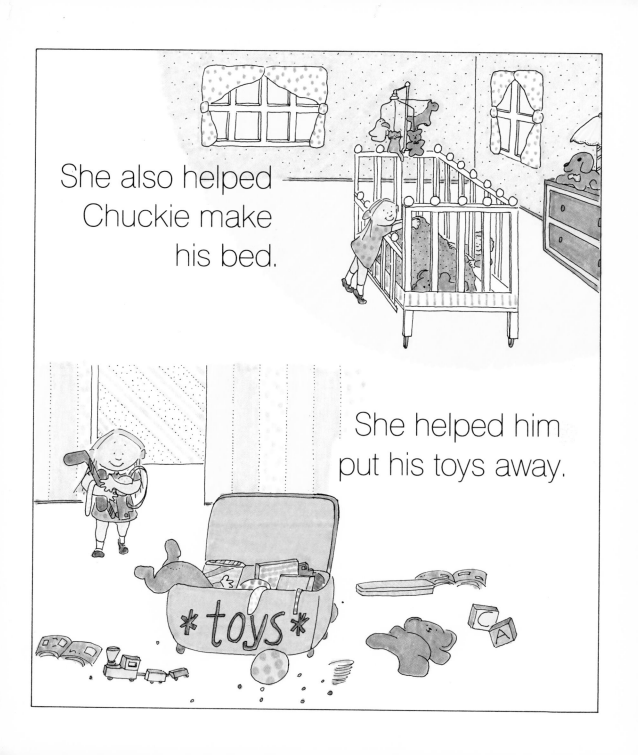

She also helped
Chuckie make
his bed.

She helped him
put his toys away.

And best of all,

she ate his carrots
for him,
sometimes

(when no one was looking).

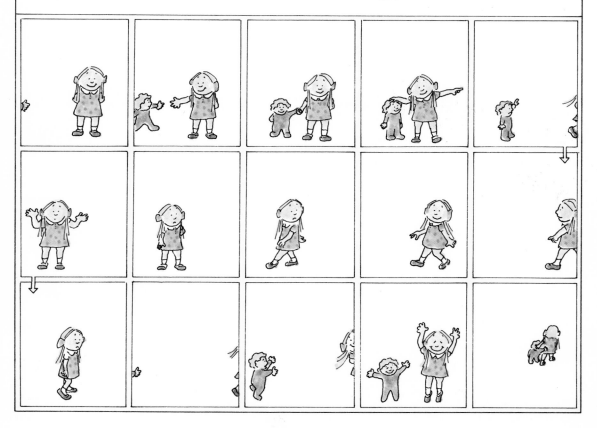